JUST A SNOWMAN

BY MERCER MAYER

To Trent Birkins

HarperFestival®

A Division of HarperCollins*Publishers*

Library of Congress catalog card number: 2003115868
A Big Tuna Trading Company, LLC/J. R. Sansevere Book
www.harperchildrens.com   www.littlecritter.com
❖
13 14 15 16 LP/CWM 20 19 18 17 16

It snowed and snowed all night long, so today we had a snow day. Hooray!

I wanted to build a snowman. I put on my snow
boots and my hat and my mittens and my scarf.

Then, I helped Little Sister
put on her snow stuff.

After that, Dad needed
my help. We shoveled and
shoveled lots of snow . . .

. . . and then we had to find the car.

I was going to build a snowman next, but Little Sister wanted to have a snowball fight. I let her hit me a bunch of times.

I only hit her one time by accident.

So then, I had to say I was sorry
and give her a big hug.

I was going to build a snowman after that, but Tiger and Bun Bun wanted to go ice-skating.

So, I showed everyone how I can skate backwards . . .

. . . and do jumps.

Then Tiger and I raced.
It was a tie.

I was ready to build a snowman next, but Maurice and Molly wanted to go sledding. I steered all the way down the big hill. Watch out, Maurice and Molly, here we come!

When Little Sister and I got home, I was going to build a snowman. But Gator wanted me to help him build a snow fort.

And then Gabby wanted to make snow angels.

Finally! It was time to build a snowman. First, we made a big snowball for the bottom.

Next, we put a smaller one on top . . .

. . . and an even smaller one on top of that one.

Little Sister added prunes for his eyes
and mouth, and a carrot for his nose.

And I put Mom's scarf around his neck and Dad's hat on his head. I even let him wear my sunglasses. Our snowman sure looked great!

Little Sister was getting cold so we went inside. The snowman looked cold, too, so I decided to make some of my special hot chocolate to warm us all up.

First, Mom heated some milk while I got out the secret ingredients.

I put everything into the pot and stirred it all up with a big spoon.

Then I put marshmallows on top and I poured the hot chocolate into three big mugs—one for me, one for Little Sister . . .

. . . and one for the snowman. It was the best snow day ever. I sure hope it snows again tomorrow!